Gold Nugget

Trip

by
CANDRI
HODGES

illustrated by
Matthew
Archambault

Thank you to my husband who patiently
endures my love of old things.

PAGES
Publishing Group ™

First printing by Willowisp Press 1998.

Published by Willowisp Press
801 94th Avenue North, St. Petersburg, Florida 33702

Printed in the United States of America

Willowisp Press ®

2 4 6 8 10 9 7 5 3 1

ISBN 0-87406-896-7

contents

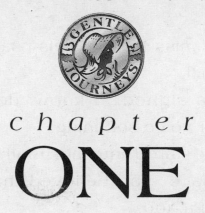

chapter
ONE

BETSY Hale sat on the coarse rag rug beside the sitting room fireplace. She rested her cheek against her mother's crisp cotton skirt.

"Please, Mama," she said, lifting her face to gaze into mother's clear, blue eyes. "Can't we just give California one more chance? Please?"

"No, Betsy." Mama folded the letter she had finished reading aloud and stuffed it into its envelope. "We've been over this before."

"But I miss Pa so," Betsy said with a small sniff.

Mama sighed. "I know, dear," she said, her voice softening.

Betsy stared into her mother's saddened face. She believed that Mama missed Pa, too.

"Mama," Betsy began again. "It's . . . it's been nearly a year since we've seen Pa. If we can't go back to stay, could we . . . could we maybe go for a visit?"

"No, Betsy," Mama said firmly. "I'll never, ever return to that dreadful wilderness!"

"But, Mama—"

"That's enough, Betsy. I'll not listen to another word." She looked at Betsy, then forced a small smile when she saw a tear slide down her daughter's cheek. "Now, I believe it's your bedtime. And here." She handed a small brown box to Betsy. "Your pa sent this for you."

Betsy took the box and tucked it into her calico skirt pocket.

"Thank you, Mama," she murmured. She got up from the rag rug, brushed another tear from her face, and bent to kiss her mother's smooth cheek.

"Goodnight," said Betsy as she slowly left the room.

*   *   *   *   *   *

Betsy quickly changed her clothes and climbed into her soft feather bed. She pulled the quilt up over her flannel nightgown and leaned back against her pillow.

She turned the small package from her pa over and over, then pried it open with her sewing scissors. Inside lay a

carefully folded letter and a shiny chunk of—it was! She lifted out and examined a heavy gold nugget in the flickering light of the candle flame.

The nugget was beautiful, and judging from its size and weight, it was probably quite valuable. But Betsy dropped it into the folds of her quilt and eagerly reached for the letter. What her pa had to say was far more important than any gift he had to give, no matter how shiny or valuable. She unfolded the letter and smoothed its creases.

June 3, 1857

My dear Betsy,

How are you? Are things going well for you and your mama in Pennsylvania?

Our small town keeps growing and growing. As a matter of fact, the entire territory of California keeps growing and growing. We have a school now and a church— two establishments that are definitely very unwilderness-like. We've also gained another hotel and a small restaurant. And, of course, two more saloons, but you know that I steer clear of those places. And best of all, the stagecoach now stops here. A small depot was built right beside the post office.

I miss you and your mama so much, Betsy. I can scarcely imagine how you must be growing. My little girl—ten years old and growing older each day, her childhood slipping swiftly past without me to share it.

Ah, but do not despair, dear. Your mama is hurt and confused, but time will heal her grief, and then I know that we will be a family once more. We must both be patient with her. Your mama is a fine woman. She simply needs to go through this difficult time in her own way. And she will, of that I am quite sure. She and I love each other very much, and I am willing to wait until she feels ready to come home. Of course, that does not lessen my missing you both, and so I will look forward to your next letter.

All my love until then,
Pa

P.S. As you can see by the enclosed gift, our gold mine is producing splendidly.

Betsy pressed the letter to her cheek and closed her eyes. She pictured her old home in California, but before another tear had a chance to form, she refolded the letter, slipped it and the gold nugget beneath her pillow, and blew out her bedside candle. She slid down deeper into the soft warmth of her feather bed. Pulling the quilt close around her neck, she closed her eyes. There was nothing she could do. Her mama's mind was set, and it was simply best to go to sleep.

chapter
TWO

BUT Betsy could not go to sleep. She squeezed her eyes shut as tightly as she could, but her mama's and grandmama's voices in the kitchen soon caught her attention. Betsy's bedroom was beside the kitchen, and every word could be heard through the walls—especially if Betsy strained to listen.

Betsy opened her eyes and quietly rolled over onto her back so both of her ears were wide open, too. She felt a little bit guilty, fooling Mama into thinking she was asleep when she had checked on her earlier. But Betsy so wanted to hear the conversation! She knew that Mama would talk about Pa's letter, and she also knew, awful as it might be for her to listen, that Mama might say things to Grandmama that she would not necessarily say to Betsy. Perhaps her mama might just admit that she missed Pa, too. Perhaps she might even consider returning home to California. Perhaps . . .

Betsy stopped her own spinning thoughts and listened to the clink of teacups and saucers and to Grand-mama dipping water from the bucket into the teapot. She heard Mama open the stove door and add a log to the crackling fire. The sound of Mama clap-clapping her hands to loosen the chips of wood bark and to clean off the bits of dirt echoed through the night air.

"I reckon you've read your letter from Edward," Grandmama said.

Mama did not answer. Betsy really could not blame Mama for her silence. She knew very well how persistent her grandmama could be.

"Is Betsy all sound asleep?" Grandmama asked. But Betsy was not fooled. Grandmama would return to the letter soon enough. She was not one to skip around a subject for too long.

"She appears to be in dreamland," Mama replied.

"Poor little lamb," Grandmama said, and Betsy smiled softly in her dark bedroom as she imagined her round grandmama firmly shaking her head, the loose clump of silver hair she called a bun swinging back and forth

against her high, lace collar.

"Land sakes, Mother," Mama said. "I suppose I'll not have any rest until I've told you every single word, sentence, and comma in the letter." Hearing the tone of her mama's voice, Betsy covered her mouth with her hand to hold in a giggle.

"The water's boiling," Grandmama answered cheerfully. And though Betsy could not hear it, she knew that her mama was spooning tea leaves into the teapot painted with pretty violets. "And, Lydia, dear," Grandmama continued, "I really am not at all sure what you mean by that. I was simply making pleasant conversation!"

"Pshaw! Pleasant conversation—oh, very well. Edward wrote what he always writes."

"That he misses you dreadfully,"

Grandmama said. "And that he hopes you will come home soon."

"I've made it perfectly clear to him that I've no intention of ever returning to that horrid place."

"Lydia, dear," Grandmama said, her voice very soft. Betsy heard the slow stirring of the spoons inside the china teacups. "You cannot continue to blame Edward or California for what has happened. It was simply life's cruel hand."

"I don't blame Edward, Mother. But I do blame California and its uncivilized conditions. Besides, Edward will come to his senses and come back East."

"I'm not so sure, Lydia," Grandmama said. "His gold claim in California and the new home he built for you are very important to him. Your husband is an adventurous man—he saw an opportunity and seized it."

"Pshaw!" Mama exclaimed again. "That silly gold mine! We don't need the money. Papa left plenty for us to live on when he died."

"Yes, he did. But Edward is proud—a good manner of proud mind you—and he needs to feel that he is providing for his family. A good man cannot bear to live off his wife's money for very long."

"Such nonsense! I love him, and my money is his money!" said Mama.

"Of course it is, dear," Grandmama agreed. "But what do you suggest Edward do if he comes back East? Your papa's business has been sold and much of the area is family farms."

"Do? Why he needn't do anything," Mama said. "Like I said, we have plenty of money."

Then Betsy heard chair legs scrape

against the wooden kitchen floor. She pictured her grandmama adding more water to the teapot.

"Besides," Mama added. "Edward loves me. We belong together, and sooner or later he'll sell that awful claim and come back home. He's simply being stubborn."

Betsy heard long skirts rustling softly as Grandmama crossed the kitchen floor. Then Betsy heard the loud bang of the teapot being set onto the black stove.

Betsy rolled over onto her side. She slid her hand up under her pillow and wrapped her fingers around the gold nugget. So Mama still loved Pa! Betsy had never dared to think differently, but sometimes she couldn't help but wonder just a tiny bit. She smiled into the darkness. There was still hope, no matter how much Mama protested. If only Betsy could do something!

"How about a slice of pound cake with your tea?" Grandmama asked sweetly.

"Yes, thank you, Mother," answered Mama.

Betsy sighed. The matter seemed to be closed. Why had Grandmama let Mama have the last word?

But Betsy did not give her grandmother enough credit. Grandmama suddenly said, "Was there anything interesting in your other letter? It was from California, too, wasn't it?"

"Really, Mother!" Mama said with a small chuckle. "You are quite impossible!"

"Hmm-hmm," Grandmama hummed innocently.

"This cake is delicious, Mother," said Mama.

"Hmm," Grandmama repeated.

"Mercy me," Mama said. "You'll not rest until you know every speck of my life!"

"Humph," Grandmama said with a loud sniff. "That's what happens when a grown married woman moves back into her old mother's house."

Mama laughed loudly.

"Hush, Lydia, you'll wake Betsy."

"Oh dear, you're right," Mama agreed, quieting down.

Betsy buried her face in her pillow to muffle her laughter. She let go of the gold nugget and brushed her tangled blond hair back from her cheek.

"Actually, my other letter *was* from California. A friend, a neighbor, writing to see how I am," answered Mama finally.

Betsy lay still and quiet. But Grand-mama didn't say another word. Several long moments passed before Mama spoke up again.

"She's concerned about Edward and me," Mama continued. "It seems an attractive young widow has moved into town and she has her eye on Edward. Of course, I'm not worried. I know that Edward will never stop loving me. But my friend felt she should write and warn me about the whole matter. She says divorce is becoming frighteningly common in the West, but she simply doesn't understand . . ."

Betsy did not hear the rest of her mama's sentence. *Divorce!* Why, di-vorce was impossible! She reached under her pillow and clutched the gold tightly in her fist. Betsy Hale had no intentions of sitting idly by while her parents divorced. Her mind raced as she formed a plan. Betsy rubbed the gold nugget, and suddenly she had the perfect idea.

Settle down and get some sleep, she told herself. *The next few days will take all the strength I have.*

Grandmama's voice drifted into Betsy's bedroom. "Please think seriously on it, Lydia," she said. "You've been away from your husband for almost a year, and Edward may grow weary, begin to doubt your love for him. He might just give up on you. Please don't let another tragedy happen to your lovely family."

"Pshaw!" Mama scoffed. "Edward knows that I love him. Before long he will come to his senses and return to Pennsylvania where he belongs."

Betsy sighed with sudden weariness,

and she soon drifted into a deep sleep.

c h a p t e r

THREE

THE next morning Betsy scrambled from her bed before the first rays of sunlight had a chance to streak across her bedroom floor. She must hurry—hurry before either her mama or grandmama awoke.

By the light of a single candle on her bedside table, Betsy grabbed her small traveling satchel, threw some of her clothes and her hairbrush inside, closed it, and snatched up her favorite rag doll. She thought for a moment, then jerked the bag open again and carefully laid her doll inside. It wouldn't do to drag her doll around—people might think she was a helpless baby. And there was certainly no room in her plan for a helpless baby.

She dressed in her best Sunday-go-to-meeting outfit. She wrapped the gold nugget in her handkerchief and tightly knotted the corners, then tucked the package deep inside her pocket. Betsy closed the pocket safely with a pin.

She scribbled a quick letter to her mama. Betsy always tried to be considerate and she did not want to worry her mama and grandmama. She wrote:

Dear Mama,

I have taken the gold nugget (my gift from Pa) to the bank for money and I'm going to

*California to visit Pa. Please don't
worry—I remember how to get
there. I love you and will see you
when I return.*

Your daughter,
Betsy

Betsy folded the letter in half and propped it against her pillow. She glanced around the room. Had she forgotten anything? Satisfied that she had everything she might need, she grabbed her satchel, blew out the candle, peeked out her bedroom doorway, crept through the still kitchen, and quietly slipped outside.

* * * * * *

What an adventure Betsy's plan turned out to be!

First, Betsy exchanged her gold into cash at the bank. Mr. Phillips, the banker, was quite impressed with the size of the nugget, and Betsy's heart swelled with pride as she explained that it had come from her Pa's very own gold mine.

She dashed to the railroad station, wanting to be on the next train to St. Louis, Missouri, before her mama found her letter and put a stop to her trip. As she sat staring out the smoky window of the train, she couldn't help but wonder at how smoothly everything was going. She remembered to purchase a ticket. No one seemed to question a young girl traveling alone as they bustled about their own business.

Of course, Betsy had told the conductor that she was going to see her
pa, and every so often he stopped to
ask if Betsy was all right. And the nice
lady with her baby sitting across from
Betsy offered her some food from the
covered basket beside her feet.

In St. Louis the stagecoach depot
was not far from the railroad station.
Betsy found it easily, but that is where
her troubles began. When she tried to
buy passage to California, she dis-
covered the cost of the ticket was far
more than she had tucked away in her
pocket.

She couldn't help herself. Huge tears
began to slide down her smoke-
smudged cheeks. She plopped down
on an empty bench and fingered a
burnt hole in her skirt. She didn't want
to get back on the dirty, spark-spitting

train. She didn't want to return to Pennsylvania—at least not now. She wanted to go to California and see Pa!

She began to sob—loud, gulping sobs that shook her whole body. What a fix she was in! Suddenly she felt a gentle hand on her shoulder and a kind voice drifted through her sobs.

"What's wrong, dear?"

Betsy looked up into the most beautiful face she had ever seen. Except for Mama's, of course. A young girl about the same age as Betsy stood at the woman's side.

"Where's your mother?" the woman asked. Betsy thought of her mama, so many miles away. She wasn't even sure if she had enough money for a train trip back to Pennsylvania. She tried to answer the nice lady, but she only cried all the more, hating herself for her weak behavior.

"She's . . . she's . . .," she choked out through her tears. She took a deep breath. "She's . . ."

Betsy's mind raced. If she told the woman her mama was in Penn-sylvania, she might send her back. And Betsy just couldn't go back—not now when she'd come this far!

Betsy sniffed loudly. "My pa . . . I've got to get to California to my pa."

"Who are you traveling with?" the woman asked.

"I'm . . . I'm alone," Betsy reluctantly admitted.

"Alone! But where is your mother?"

"She's . . ." A left-over sob escaped from Betsy. To her own embarrass-ment, Betsy hiccuped loudly.

"I think I understand," the woman said softly, a sympathetic look on her

face. "Well, do you have a ticket?"

"N-n-no," Betsy replied. She wasn't sure what the woman understood, but at least she hadn't asked about her mama again. "I-I haven't enough money. Pa sent me some gold, but it's not enough . . . and . . . and I don't know what to do."

"Dreadful," the woman muttered quietly. "Simply dreadful! A father who can't travel to pick up his motherless child. Simply dreadful. Why, if this was my own Margaret . . ." She shook her head.

Betsy didn't quite know what to say so she didn't say anything at all. And from that point on, the kind woman, Mrs. Staton, took Betsy under her wing.

She insisted on paying for Betsy's trip and she fussed over Betsy in the same manner as she did her own daughter, Margaret. She pointed out interesting sights along the trail: herds of buffalo grazing on the long prairie grass, sod houses with wildflowers sprouting from the roofs, and even a small band of Indian braves riding in the distance.

Mrs. Staton made sure that Betsy had plenty to eat and that she washed away the black prairie dust that clung to her. And one evening, when a swarm of pesky mosquitoes nibbled endlessly at the stage travelers, Mrs. Staton smeared a smelly, gritty paste of vinegar and salt on both Betsy and Margaret!

Finally, Betsy arrived in California, safe and sound. After thanking them several times, Betsy parted from Mrs. Staton and Margaret in San Francisco, assuring them that she would be fine for the final short distance of her trip. Still, Betsy noticed that Mrs. Staton had a long talk with the stagecoach driver, and she was fairly certain that she was the subject of Mrs. Staton's no-nonsense discussion.

Several hours later, Betsy stood on the porch of the very same stagecoach depot her pa had written about. How close she was to her old home and her pa. She could hardly wait to see them both!

chapter

FOUR

BETSY straightened her soiled bonnet, picked up her traveling bag, and leaped from the top step of the stagecoach depot porch. She glanced next door to the post office. Betsy spotted Mrs. Flint, the postmistress, and she waved pleasantly at her. Mrs. Flint lowered her chin and stared over her spectacles at Betsy. Then with a small disbelieving shake of her head, she returned Betsy's wave.

Betsy stared all around her. The town looked so familiar, but there were some obvious changes. The new buildings her pa had written about caught her eye, especially the restaurant. Her stomach grumbled, but Betsy ignored it. She hadn't time to dawdle. She would eat something at home.

Home! How wonderful that sounded! A small bird hopped across the dirt street, pausing inside a dusty wheel rut to peck at a bug. Betsy thought about the robin's nest in the eave of her grandmama's porch roof. That only made her think of her grandmama. And Mama.

Perhaps Mama is worried about me, Betsy thought. It seemed strange to consider that nearly a month had passed since Betsy had left her Pennsylvania home. By now Mama would surely have realized that Betsy was fine. After all, Betsy had left a perfectly good note, hadn't she?

Betsy side-stepped a pile of horse manure and continued along the street. People bustled up and down the wooden sidewalk into stores, the blacksmith shop, and the livery stable. Several women and one man recognized Betsy, stopped and gave her a second look and then a hearty wave. Betsy smiled and waved to each of them in return.

Perhaps I'll see one of my old friends, she thought hopefully. *Eliza or Annie or perhaps my best friend Frances Mae.*

But as she hurried along the town street, she did not meet anyone else she knew. Betsy soon came to the outskirts of town.

"Just a little ways to Pa's claim," she whispered excitedly. She was glad for her good memory. She knew exactly which way to go. Over two hills, across the stream, and along the Larsons' pasture fence. And suddenly, as she turned a small curve at the edge of the Larsons' farm, there it was, exactly as she remembered it.

She stood perfectly still for a moment, staring at the rugged log cabin. Home! Large tears welled up, stinging her eyes. A year was such a very long time to be away, and yet, now that she was here, it seemed as though she'd never left. Her rope swing still dangled from the huge oak near the chicken coop, and a tidy stack of wood stood beside the heavy wooden cabin door. And behind that door— behind that door was her pa!

She clutched her satchel, tore off her dusty bonnet, and raced across the field, the breeze blowing through her long, blond hair. How surprised Pa would be to see her! At the thought of seeing his bright eyes and hearing his hearty laughter, Betsy pushed forward as fast as her legs would take her.

"Pa!" Betsy shouted. She scrambled onto the narrow porch and burst through the front doorway.

"Pa! It's me—Betsy. I've come to see you." She paused in the sitting room as silence greeted her. "Pa?"

She wandered into the small kitchen. The black cookstove was cold. She raced into her parents' bedroom, and finding the same silence, she hurried into her own. She stood for a long time, staring. Her old bedroom. It was exactly as she had left it. The bunk her pa had built from rough logs was neatly made up with her pink and blue quilt. A candle stub still sat in a holder on her bedside table. And an empty toy cradle rested in the corner.

Betsy set her bag on the bed and opened it. Reaching inside, she took out her rag doll and then gently placed it in the cradle. She tucked the patch-work quilt around the doll's shoulders, placed a quick kiss on the cloth fore-head, turned, and hurried out the door.

She ran out the kitchen door into the backyard.

"Pa!" she shouted once more. "Pa?"

And then she realized where he was. Of course! Pa was probably working at the claim. Gold did not jump out of the thick rocks and sparkling streams by itself. She briefly thought about going to the claim and searching for Pa, but then she remembered his serious warnings that she should never, ever go there by herself—any number of accidents could happen.

Well, he would be back by supper time. And Betsy could wait. After all, what was a few more hours after nearly a year? She would settle in, unpack her clothes, and rest a bit.

Betsy's stomach grumbled again. Oh, yes, and get a bite to eat. But first . . . first there was a place she must visit—a place she longed to see.

c h a p t e r

FIVE

BETSY walked slowly through the backyard toward a small clump of bushes. Beside the bushes was a short fence. Betsy slipped through an opening at one corner of the fence. The area was small, a tiny square in the middle of her mama and papa's property.

She quietly knelt beside a carefully carved wooden cross. She reached out and touched the petals of a bright geranium growing beside the cross. Of course, her pa had lovingly planted the flower as well as the row of wild roses that lined the inside of the fence.

She already knew the name on the cross, but she took the time to read it again.

Aaron James Hale
Born May 7, 1855
Died June 29, 1856
Aged 1 year, 1 month, 22 days

Here was the reason Mama had crumbled before their eyes. Here was the reason Mama had taken Betsy and had fled back East. Here was the reason Mama could not bear to live in California. Aaron James Hale was Betsy's baby brother, and here was his tiny, tragic grave. He had died from cholera during a brief epidemic that swept through the small town. Others died, too, but that did little to lessen the Hale family's grief.

Mama clearly blamed California for her baby's death. When they had first moved West, Pa had assured Mama that the air was fresh and clean and free of disease, unlike the crowded East.

Betsy was six years old then, and she remembered much of the long, slow covered wagon trip across the country. When Betsy was eight, her baby brother was born and the Hale family was delighted. Their life was not always easy—Pa worked hard at the gold claim and Mama worked the rich ground to grow vegetables. Together they raised a small herd of cows and enough chickens for eggs. No, life was not always easy, but it was always happy and full of love. Until little Aaron's death.

When the tragedy struck, Mama refused to go on as usual. She shouted at Pa and sometimes Betsy could still hear Mama's words ringing in her head.

"Where is all that clean, undiseased air, Edward? Certainly I cannot stay here in this child-stealing land." And then she would break down and cry and Mama's heart-breaking sobs were harder for Betsy to bear than her angry words. Soon after little Aaron was laid to rest in the dry, hard ground, Mama packed up and she and Betsy headed East on the next stagecoach. Betsy still remembered the tears in her pa's eyes and the pleading in his voice, but Mama stubbornly gathered her skirts and climbed into the stagecoach.

"You know where to find us, Edward," she said firmly. "I love you but I cannot stay here another day." She gazed down at her husband, and Betsy could see the sadness in her face. "Please come to Pennsylvania with us."

But Pa shook his head and said, "This is our home, Lydia. I'll always be here, waiting for you."

Betsy had stared out the stagecoach window, watching as Pa grew smaller and smaller in the distance until he was a tiny speck, and then, finally, he disappeared from sight.

Now, kneeling beside her baby brother's grave, Betsy shook her head to clear away the memories. She had come to visit Pa. This was a happy time and she would not cloud it with the past. She stood but leaned down close to the wooden cross one more time.

"I miss you, Aaron," Betsy whispered, remembering his soft golden curls, his large brown eyes, his crooked grin, and the funny way he stamped his foot when he wanted Betsy to pay attention to him.

She brushed bits of dirt from her hands and skirt. She bent to smell the wild roses and then quietly slipped through the fence opening.

Back inside the kitchen, Betsy rummaged until she found a loaf of bread and a small jug of honey. When she had finished eating, she took the water bucket outside, filled it with fresh spring water, and returned to the kitchen. She poured some of the cool water into a tin mug and drank it quickly, enjoying the clean taste after so many days of questionable water on the stagecoach trail.

Now what? she thought, glancing up at the clock on the fireplace mantel. Pa probably would not return for several hours. Betsy nibbled the end of her finger, wondering what she could do to fill the time.

There was one rather important chore she needed to do. She supposed that now was as good a time as any. She went into her bedroom, gathered all her dusty, smelly clothes from her bag, and headed out the door. As an afterthought, she returned to the bedroom and removed the dress from her rag doll. She stared at the doll, its cloth body clean but its face, arms, and legs speckled with dust. Betsy tucked the doll into the pile of clothes and headed to the kitchen. There she searched until she found a block of yellow homemade soap, then left the house and made her way to the wide stream that ran between the apple trees her pa and mama had planted a couple of years before.

Betsy dunked the first dress into the cold, rushing stream. It was her favorite dress, pale blue with tiny red flowers. Clutching the block of soap, she scrubbed the dress, then rinsed and laid it aside. Grabbing the rest of the clothes, she plunged them beneath the clear water. She rubbed in more soap until a bubbly circle of lather formed on the water's surface and clung to the smooth rocks that lined the stream's banks.

Betsy suddenly giggled and held up a sudsy blouse. *Wouldn't Mama have a fit?* she thought. *Washing my clothes in a cold stream instead of in boiling water in a proper wooden washtub!* She scooped up some bubbles and blew them into the bright sunshine.

Reaching into the stream, she swished the clothes free of the soap. After wringing them as best she could, she hung them to dry across the washline strung between the apple trees.

She lay back in the soft grass and gazed at the brilliant blue sky. A soft puffy cloud floated by and Betsy giggled again. This was the very best idea she had ever had. Pa would come home, she would beg him to come to Pennsylvania to talk to Mama, and everything would be as it should.

She bit her lower lip. She hoped that Mama would not be too angry. After all, Betsy realized that even though she had left a note, she hadn't exactly asked Mama's permission to come to California. She sat up and shrugged. Oh, well, what was done was done.

Glancing down at the dress she

wore, Betsy saw that it too was dirty. She slipped out of her clothes down to her chemise and scrubbed away their dirt. Then she jumped into the stream, splashing and running through the chilly water. She shampooed her hair and scrubbed her skin until it tingled.

Pa would find a squeaky clean daughter when he returned home that evening!

chapter
SIX

BETSY laid aside the storybook she had been reading. The summer breeze had quickly dried her clothes, and she felt better wearing clean garments after such a long trip. She flounced her skirt a bit, proud of the job she had done.

Betsy glanced at the mantel clock. Surely Pa would be coming soon. She stared out the window, then wandered out the front door.

The late afternoon sun had begun to

drop until it seemed to be cradled among the tips of the towering trees. Betsy leaned against a porch post, drinking in the beauty of the wide, open countryside.

Suddenly she heard a faint clanging of tin pails coming from the chicken coop.

Pa!

She raced across the yard, her bare feet churning up swirling puffs of dust. She burst through the coop doorway. But the person who turned to stare at her, his mouth open wide, was not her pa.

"Who are you?" the tall boy demanded.

"That's what *I'd* like to know," Betsy replied. "Who are you?"

"I asked first," the boy shot back. He pushed a thick lock of dark hair off his forehead.

Betsy put her hands on her hips, her eyes narrowed. She tilted her head and studied the strange boy. He seemed to be working, helping Pa.

"I'm Betsy," she finally said.

"Mr. Hale's daughter?"

"Yep."

The boy grinned. "Well, I'll be," he said. "You really did come back like your pa said. I'm Marty—Marty Cates. I live at the next farm over. Your pa asked me to feed the chickens and milk the cow." He pointed absently off in the distance.

Betsy couldn't help but smile. "Pa told you about me?"

"Oh, sure, he talks about you and your ma all the time." Marty glanced toward the log cabin. "Your ma in the house?"

"No . . ."

"Well, where is she? Your pa will be right happy," Marty said. He walked out of the chicken coop and began to scatter chicken feed over the ground.

Betsy hesitated. Should she tell this stranger the truth? He seemed nice enough. Besides, her pa trusted him to come over and help with the chores. She followed him outside. After all, he was her neighbor, wasn't he?

"She's . . . she's in Pennsylvania," Betsy said.

"So, who did you come with?"

"No one. I came by myself." Well, that was the truth. Never mind that she'd had help from Mrs. Staton.

Marty's head jerked up and he turned around to stare at Betsy.

"Balderdash!" he said firmly. "Ain't no way a girl could come clear across the country by herself." He stepped closer and eyed Betsy. "How old are you?"

Betsy straightened to her full height. Now she was really glad she had not told him about Mrs. Staton.

"I'm nearly eleven! And I *did* come by myself. I'm not a baby, you know," she answered indignantly.

"All right, all right," Marty said. "You don't have to get yourself in a pucker." He glanced around the yard and toward the house once more. "I s'pose you might've come alone." He returned to his chicken feed, but slowly shook his head. "Seems mighty hard to believe though," he muttered.

Betsy crossed her arms, her mouth set in a firm, straight line. After several long, quiet moments she asked, "Where's my pa?"

Marty looked up. "He went to have his gold weighed. I don't expect him back for . . .," Marty paused and silently counted on his fingers. "For three more days," he finished.

"Oh, no!" Betsy couldn't believe her awful luck. To come all this way, and then find out that Pa had gone off on a trip!

Marty eyed Betsy. "Can't be helped. I reckon you'll just have to come home with me. My ma will be glad for your company till your pa comes back."

Betsy chewed her lower lip. This would never do. She simply couldn't go home with Marty. She had come so far and she intended to be here when Pa returned.

"That's . . . that's mighty nice of you," she said, "but I can't do that. I've got to stay and wait for Pa."

"Humph," Marty grunted. "I can't let you stay here by yourself. My ma would have a fit!"

"Oh, please," Betsy pleaded. "You don't have to tell her I'm here, do you?"

"Lie to my folks?" asked Marty.

"Well, no, . . . not lie. Just don't mention me at all," Betsy said.

Marty gave her a hard look. "I don't know."

"I'll be fine," Betsy argued. "Really." She studied Marty for a second. "How old are *you*?" she asked.

"Eleven," he replied. "My birthday was two months ago. Why?"

Betsy smiled a broad smile. "See there? We're almost the same age. You could stay by yourself for three days, couldn't you?"

Marty began to pour water into the chickens' tin water pans. "Well, sure," he said over his shoulder. "But I'm older than you."

"Pooh. By a few months," said Betsy.

"Besides," Marty scoffed. "I'm a fella."

"What's that have to do with anything?" Betsy demanded, her face flushing with anger.

"Everything."

"Oh, pooh," Betsy said again. "I mean, I got all the way across the United States, didn't I?"

Marty set down the water pail and grinned. "I reckon you did at that," he said.

"Oh, Marty," Betsy said. "I just have to be here when Pa comes home. It's been so long since I've seen him."

"All right," Marty said. "I'll keep your secret. I can bring you some food," he offered.

"No, thank you. I'll be fine. I've got eggs and bread and there are vegetables in Pa's garden. What have you been doing with Pa's milk?"

"He told me to take it on home to Ma—it would just spoil till he got back. You want me to leave a little for you?" Marty asked.

Betsy nodded.

"I'd best keep coming every day, though," Marty said. "Ma and Pa might get suspicious if I don't do your pa's chores."

Betsy nodded again and then she grinned. "That's good thinking." She looked at Marty. He really was a nice boy. Perhaps they could be friends. It would be fun to have a new friend when she and Mama moved back to California. Of course, Pa might decide to go live in Pennsylvania. Well, whatever happened, the important thing was to reunite her parents. But for now at least, she and Marty might be friends.

"Besides," Marty said, returning Betsy's grin, "I'd best come on over and check on you, too."

Betsy crossed her arms and glared at Marty. Then again, it seemed as if he was going to be a mighty bossy friend!

chapter

SEVEN

ONLY one word could describe Betsy's first full day at the cabin. Boring.

Betsy awoke as a flash of lightning brightened her dim bedroom. Burrowing down beneath her pink and blue quilt, she closed her eyes and tried to go back to sleep. A clap of thunder split the silence, and Betsy sighed and crawled from her cozy bed.

After several frustrating tries, she finally built a fire in the black cookstove. She was glad her mama had taught her how to work in the kitchen. She cooked a kettle of porridge, which she ate for breakfast, and hard-boiled some eggs for dinner.

She puttered about the house, doing this and that, sweeping the floors, dusting the fireplace mantel, and washing the dishes. She pushed a chair close to the fireplace mantel, climbed up, and carefully wound the clock with its special key. She couldn't bear it if the clock stopped and she didn't know the time. All the while, lightning flashed, thunder rumbled, and a steady rain beat against the log cabin.

Betsy patted herself on the back for having been clever enough to carry several pails of water from the spring the evening before. Going outside in the storm would have been a most unpleasant chore. Finally, the rain slowed and then stopped as the last bit of thunder rolled off into the distance. The afternoon sun peeked through the clouds. Betsy took a newspaper she found on the fireplace mantel outside to the porch. Never mind that the news was several weeks old—reading it would pass time.

She was halfway through the newspaper when Marty appeared. Betsy was so happy to see him! She chattered as he fed the chickens and milked the cow. She talked as he refilled her water pails. She rambled on as he handed her a small bundle tied up inside a soft, clean towel.

"Here," Marty said. "I brought you some biscuits and a hunk of ham."

"Oh, thank you," Betsy said. She tore

open the bundle and broke off a chunk of biscuit. ". . . and then I heard Mama tell Grandmama about some widow lady that's got her eye on Pa," she continued as she ate. She had already told Marty all about losing her baby brother, moving back to Pennsylvania, and Pa sending her the gold nugget. "So I just had to come—to see if I could fix things."

"Hmm," Marty said. They sat down on the top step of the porch. Marty reached over and took a biscuit. "That lady would be the Widow Evans. Now that you mention it, she has been mighty friendly to your pa."

"Why, of all the—!" Betsy said with a scowl. "Doesn't she know about me and Mama?"

Marty shrugged. "I reckon so. But knowing and seeing are two different things." He looked at Betsy and grinned. "I knew all about you, but seeing you is nothing like I expected." He slapped his knee and laughed.

Betsy gave him a little shove, then reached down for a piece of ham. She chewed it slowly, thoughtfully.

"Is she . . . is the Widow Evans pretty?" she asked.

Marty shrugged again. "I s'pose so. If you like the fussy type."

Betsy didn't say anything. She didn't know what type Pa liked. All she knew was that he liked Mama's type.

Marty stood and brushed the biscuit crumbs from his hands. He picked up his pail of milk. "I'd best be heading home before my folks wonder what's keeping me." He looked at Betsy. "Are you sure you're all right here?"

"Yes, yes," Betsy replied absently.

She waved her hand, her mind still on the Widow Evans. "I'll see you to-morrow."

"All right," Marty said. "Don't forget to lock the house up tight tonight."

"Um-hmm." Betsy nodded. Now she was sure she had done the right thing. She could scarcely wait for Pa to come home.

*   *   *   *   *   *

Betsy's second day was the opposite of her first day. The summer sun streamed through her mama's muslin curtains and streaked the wooden floor.

Betsy fried a batch of griddle cakes and smothered them with honey. *One more day!* she thought. *One more day and Pa will be home!*

The morning passed quietly. Betsy found a piece of half-finished embroidery that her mama had left behind. She worked on it most of the morning. Her stitches were not nearly as neat as Mama's, but they would have to do. The mantel clock struck twelve o'clock, and Betsy's stomach began to grumble for dinner. As she laid aside her needlework, she heard a gentle knock on the front door.

Was it Marty? She doubted it—it was too early. Besides, he'd just poke his head at the window and holler her name. Suddenly Betsy had an uneasy thought. What if Marty had changed his mind and told his mother about Betsy? Betsy put her hands on her hips and her mouth tightened into a straight line. If he did . . . after he had promised . . .

The knock came again, a bit louder.

Betsy hurried to the door. She opened it quickly.

"Mr. Hale, it's such a lovely—" The woman standing there stopped short. She glanced down into Betsy's wide, blue eyes. "Oh, hello," she said. She was dressed in a pale pink dress trimmed with layers of lace. Her bonnet was made of the same pink cloth and was edged with the same delicate lace. Wisps of dark hair curled from beneath the rim of the bonnet. She peered over Betsy's left shoulder. "Is Mr. Hale here?"

"Not at the moment," Betsy said. She cleared her throat. "Who are you?"

"I'm Mrs. Evans. And you are . . .?"

Betsy's eyes narrowed. The Widow Evans! Why was she here? Betsy glanced down at the cloth-covered basket looped over the Widow Evans's arm. She frowned. It looked like a picnic basket.

Betsy looked up into the woman's soft, gray eyes.

"I'm Betsy, Mr. Hale's daughter," she said firmly.

"Really!" The woman suddenly seemed confused. "But I thought . . . is your mother here?"

"No, . . . not at the moment."

The woman glanced over Betsy's shoulder again. Her gaze rested briefly on the embroidered cloth. She looked back at Betsy.

"I see," she said.

She thinks Mama came here with me, Betsy thought, and a small smile lifted the corners of her mouth. *Good!*

"I'm . . . I'm sorry I troubled you," the Widow Evans said. "I'll just be on my way."

"No trouble at all," Betsy said, a little

too cheerfully. She watched as the woman left the porch, climbed into a small carriage, and drove away.

Betsy closed the front door, leaning against it while she sorted out her thoughts. Obviously the widow *did* have her eye on Pa. Why else would she appear with a picnic basket? But, of course, she didn't know that Pa wasn't home. That surely meant that he didn't discuss his plans with her. If they were close friends, she not only would have known he was gone, but she probably would have known *where* he had gone. And didn't she call Pa "Mr. Hale," not "Edward" as Mama called him? That surely meant something, too.

Betsy smiled softly. No, the Widow Evans was simply doing some wishful thinking. Pa still loved Mama—that was plain to see just by looking around the house. Mama's crystal vase still stood on the mantel. Mama's garden shawl was still hanging on its hook beside the back door. Mama's favorite teacup still sat on the kitchen shelf. And the frilly pillow stitched with Mama and Pa's wedding date was still secure in the corner of the old sitting room rocking chair.

"Yes," Betsy said out loud so the truth filled the whole cabin. "Pa still loves Mama." And she hugged herself at the thought.

chapter
EIGHT

BETSY clung with one hand to her rope swing, swaying slowly back and forth as she nibbled a fresh, crisp carrot from her pa's garden. It was a lovely summer day, bright and breezy. Betsy couldn't bear to stay inside. More importantly, she was waiting for Pa—today was the day he would return from his trip.

A busy squirrel scampered across the yard and up a tree. It chattered at Betsy, seeming to scold her for her idleness.

Betsy giggled and popped the last bite of a carrot into her mouth. She wrapped her legs tighter around the rope swing, her feet resting on the thick knot near the bottom. Clutching the coarse rope between her hands, she leaned her head back—way, way back until her long, blond braids nearly brushed the ground.

Then Betsy heard steady hoofbeats in the distance. She straightened and stared at the single rider coming, a small cloud of dust swirling around the horse's legs.

"Pa," she whispered.

Betsy couldn't seem to move. She clung to the swing, frozen in place.

The rider galloped up to the barn. He glanced at the rope swing and then looked away. He jerked his head around again. His eyes widened with disbelief. Edward Hale leaped from his saddle and raced across the yard.

And then Betsy came back to life. She dropped to the ground and pushed her legs as fast as they would move, shouting, "Pa! Pa!" as she ran. She flew into Pa's arms. He scooped her up and hugged her close, tears streaming down his cheeks.

"Betsy, Betsy, is it really you?" he asked, laughing. He held her at arm's length to gaze at her, then pulled her back again for another hug. "I can't believe it," he said. "You've finally come. You're the best thing I've seen in ever so long."

He firmly set her aside and stood. "Where's your mama?" he asked. He began to walk, then burst into a full run toward the log cabin.

"Lydia!" he shouted. "Lydie, where are you? Lydie! Lydie!"

Betsy scurried after him. She chased him through the yard and into the sitting room.

"Pa!" Betsy said.

But Pa didn't seem to hear her. He raced into the bedroom and then the kitchen. "Lydia!" he shouted.

Betsy followed her pa through the pantry and into the backyard. "Pa," she said again, a bit louder.

But Pa still didn't listen. He ran to the chicken coop and then into the barn. "Lydie," he cried. "Are you in here?"

Betsy finally caught her pa. She grabbed his hand.

"Pa," she pleaded.

He slowly looked down at her.

"She's . . . she's not here, Pa."

"Well, girl, then where is she?" he

asked, his dark eyes shining with happy tears and excitement. "Is she over to see the Larsons? Gone into town?"

Betsy bit her bottom lip. She dropped her pa's hand and took several steps. She reached out and patted the cow's nose.

"I . . . I . . ."

"Yes?" Pa asked.

"Pa, Mama's still in Pennsylvania," Betsy blurted out. "I came alone."

Pa's eyes widened in disbelief, then narrowed with suspicion.

"I reckon you'd best say that again," he said, tilting his head to study Betsy. "I don't believe I heard you correctly."

Betsy squirmed beneath his stare. This wasn't going at all the way she had planned.

"I . . . I . . .," she stammered. She

took a deep breath. "Mama's still in Pennsylvania," she repeated, letting out her breath in a single rush. "I came alone."

"What?!" Pa yelled. "Has your mama lost her mind? Why, you're way too young. Doesn't she realize the dangers—"

He suddenly paled as the anger swiftly drained from his face. He grabbed Betsy's shoulders and stared into her wide eyes. "Is your mama all right? Has something happened? Oh, I never should have agreed to this separation."

"No, Pa, no," Betsy cried, trying to break through his frantic rush of words. "Mama's fine. It's just that . . ."

Relieved that his worst fears had not come to pass, Pa settled down as quickly as he had panicked.

"It's just that what?" he asked, looking directly at his daughter who still had some explaining to do.

"It's just that I . . . I missed you," Betsy said.

Pa pulled Betsy to him and hugged her so hard Betsy could scarcely breathe. "Oh, Betsy, I missed you, too. You'll never know how very much I missed you."

He let go of Betsy and stepped back. "And I must say, I'm right happy to see you, too!" He gave her one of the hearty smiles she remembered so well. "Now, what's this nonsense about coming by yourself? Why on earth would your mama agree to such a thing? And why didn't she write me about your trip?"

"Well, she didn't really agree," Betsy admitted meekly.

Pa crossed his arms and Betsy noticed that his brow was creased in disapproval. "Betsy . . .," he said, and that one word was enough.

Betsy began to talk—fast. She told him about everything, from eaves-dropping on her mama and grand-mama, to cashing in the gold nugget, to the dirty train ride, to the long dusty stagecoach trip, and even to her last few days at the log cabin by herself.

"I left Mama a note," she said softly as she ended her tale.

Her pa stood quietly, thoughtfully listening the whole time Betsy spoke. Betsy could not quite read the ex-pression on his face. She held her breath, waiting for his reaction. She was in big trouble; she just knew it.

Pa bent his head and stood staring at the barn floor.

He's too mad to talk, Betsy thought. *I'm really going to get it. And I suppose I have it coming. This is the stupidest thing I've ever done. Poor Mama is probably worried out of her mind.*

Betsy hadn't thought that Mama would worry too much, but now, after talking with Pa, she realized her mistake.

But as Betsy waited, she couldn't help but argue with her conscience. *No, I'm still glad I came,* she thought. *Even if he's mad, it's so good to see Pa.*

But the longer he stared at the floor, the more nervous Betsy grew. Why didn't he scold or punish her? *Or something?* Although only a minute had passed, to Betsy it seemed to last forever.

She was definitely in deep trouble.

c h a p t e r

NINE

FIRST Betsy stood perfectly still and waited. Then she shifted from one foot to the other. Then she stood still again until finally, she could bear it no longer.

"Pa!" she blurted. "Say something. Please!"

Then she noticed the slight shake of her pa's shoulders. She heard his soft chuckle that grew and grew until he threw back his head and laughed long and loud.

He looked at Betsy, his eyes twinkling. He reached out and took Betsy's hand, squeezing it tightly.

"Girl," he said between a few stray chuckles, "I know right well I should be downright furious with you."

Betsy squeezed her pa's hand in return and smiled sheepishly. She knew that if her pa began a sentence with those words, he was more than likely not furious.

Pa shook his head and continued. "I should be so very furious," he said, and he reached out and held Betsy's face between his big hands. "But I'm not," he admitted with a grin. "The truth be told, I'm so happy to see you and so very relieved that you're safe." His face turned serious and he shook his head again. "When I think what could have— No." He shook his head again. "I won't think about it."

He frowned at Betsy. "Happy or not, don't think that I approve of your little adventure. Your mama must be worried sick. You and I are heading right back into town to buy tickets for the next stagecoach east. You're going home, young lady."

Betsy smiled widely at his words. This was working just as she planned. Pa would take her back home, talk to Mama . . .

"No, Betsy," Pa said quickly, interrupting Betsy's thoughts. "I don't know what's going on inside that head of yours, but I'm not going to Pennsylvania with you. I'll take you as far as St. Louis, and then I'm putting you on the train. The conductor will keep a watch on you. You're going back home to your mama and grandmama."

Betsy knew better than to argue. She sighed softly. She would wait. Perhaps Pa would change his mind on the stagecoach trip. Perhaps, if she talked and talked about Mama . . .

"C'mon, Betsy," Pa said. He lifted her chin, gave her a gentle smile, and then turned and headed for the cabin.

*　*　*　*　*　*

After Pa cleaned up from his trip, he hitched his horse to the buckboard wagon and they rode directly to the stagecoach depot.

"Sorry, folks," the station master said. "Your timing couldn't have been worse. The stage just pulled out half an hour ago. Won't be another one for three days."

"Well," Pa said slowly, "I reckon it

can't be helped. I'll take two passages."
He reached into his pants pocket. "You
accept gold?"

"Surely," the station master replied,
sliding the scales across the counter.

Three more days in California! Betsy
couldn't keep herself from grinning.
Three days before they had to get on
that dusty, bumpy stagecoach. Three
wonderful days at home with Pa!

"Betsy," Pa scolded quietly, seeing
the grin on her face. He reached out
and accepted the stagecoach tickets.
He glanced back at Betsy and shook
his head, chuckling softly.

"Thank you kindly, sir. See you in
three days." He touched the brim of his
hat to the station master.

Betsy giggled and skipped down the
wooden depot steps.

Pa stood on the edge of the porch

and watched her. Betsy turned and waited for Pa. He shoved his hands into his pants pockets and slowly followed her down the steps. He stopped on the street and gazed up one side of the dusty rutted street and down the other side. He looked down at Betsy and smiled. He put his arm around her shoulders and hugged her close.

"Well, girl," he said, his eyes twinkling. "I suppose we'd best make the most of it. How about if I show you all the changes in town?"

Betsy nodded and she felt that her heart would burst with joy. "I'd like that, Pa," she said softly.

"All right. And when we're all finished, we'll eat at the restaurant. Mrs. Beadle makes a dandy pot roast and fixin's. How's that sound?"

Betsy's eyes widened with excitement.

How did that sound? It sounded absolutely perfect.

*   *   *   *   *   *

Betsy leaned back against the smooth, wooden wagon seat.

"I am so full, Pa. That pot roast was delicious," she said.

Pa laughed at Betsy. "Not to mention those three jelly tarts and the slice of dried apple cake you gobbled up."

Betsy grinned sheepishly, then laughed. "And it was such fun to see Frances Mae," she said. "I haven't any friends in Pennsylvania that match Frances Mae."

"So you had a good time?" Pa asked.

"It was wonderful, Pa."

Pa tugged gently on the reins as they pulled up to the barn. "Whoa,

whoa," he called to the horses.

"Do you want to go see the mine?" he asked, turning to Betsy, who nodded in reply. "Help me with Henry first," he said.

When they had finished tending the horse, Betsy raced ahead of Pa, heading around the back of the log cabin toward the gold claim.

"I'll race you," she shouted, laughing as she ran.

But when she reached the backyard, she stopped abruptly. She heard Pa run up behind her. For a moment, silence filled the warm summer air as father and daughter stared in disbelief.

Finally Pa spoke, his voice scarcely above a whisper.

"Lydia."

"Mama," Betsy echoed quietly. And then she shouted and began to run as fast as she could. "Mama! Mama!"

She heard her Pa's feet pounding beside her, and then suddenly he was in front of her. She heard his shouts above her own.

"Lydia! Lydie!" Pa called.

They both ran through the opening of the small fence—the fence that encircled baby Aaron's grave. Betsy stopped and stood still, watching as Pa pulled Mama into his arms, lifting her feet off the green grass and spinning her around. He lowered her gently and kissed her—a kiss that made Betsy hug herself with happiness.

She knew it! Mama and Pa *did* love each other. Pa ended the kiss and Betsy could see tears streaming down Mama's face.

She ran to Mama and threw her arms around her waist. Mama turned to her

and hugged her so tightly it hurt, but Betsy didn't mind the squeezing pain.

"Oh, Betsy, Betsy," Mama cried as more tears flowed down her cheeks. "You're all right. You're all right."

And then she released Betsy and set her at arm's length.

"Betsy Hale, don't you ever, ever do anything like this again! Why, I've a good mind to turn you over my knee right this instant and tan your backside good!" And then she pulled Betsy close again and burst into a fresh batch of tears. "If anything had happened to you," she whispered against Betsy's ear. She smoothed her hand against Betsy's hair. "If anything . . . I . . . I just couldn't have borne it."

Pa put his arms around Mama and Betsy and gently led them out through the fence's opening. Mama wiped her eyes with her lace handkerchief and smiled at Pa and then at Betsy.

"It's so good to see you, Lydie," Pa said. "I've dreamed of this moment more times than I can count. I was beginning to think you might never come home."

"Why, Edward," Mama replied. "How could I *not* come? I had to find Betsy. I had to make sure she got back to Pennsylvania safe and sound."

"So you intend to return to your mother's?" Pa asked.

"Edward, I . . ." Mama turned from Pa and looked down at Betsy. "The next stagecoach leaves in three days, Betsy. We have to go. Your grandmama will be worried."

Betsy stared up at her mother, her eyes wide with disbelief. Whatever was Mama saying? She couldn't possibly mean to go back to Pennsylvania! Not when they were all finally together again!

Why wasn't this going as Betsy had planned?

chapter
TEN

THE silence hung heavy in the warm summer air. A small bird swooped down, its cry piercing the quiet heat as the Hales slowly made their way to the log cabin.

Mama cleared her throat. "Tomorrow morning we'll go to town and purchase two passages home," she said firmly.

"No need," Pa said through gritted teeth. "We've just come from there. I already bought two passes."

Betsy frowned. Why was Pa making it

so easy? She didn't want to return to her grandmama's—she wanted to stay here. And she wanted Mama to stay, too.

"Very well," Mama said softly.

Suddenly Pa stopped walking. He crossed his arms and stared at Mama.

"Now, Lydia," he said. "Don't be in such an all-fired hurry. I think it's best if we discuss this situation."

"Nothing's changed, Edward," Mama replied.

"I agree," said Pa. "You're just as stubborn as always."

"Edward!" Mama exclaimed.

Pa grasped Mama's arm and looked straight into her eyes.

"Lydie," he said firmly, "you know it's true. And something else hasn't changed either. We love each other, and we've got to find a solution for this unbearable situation." He took Mama's hand and smiled softly at her. "Don't you miss me, Lydie? Just a little?"

Mama sighed. "Of course, I do. You're my husband. But, Edward, I cannot stay in California." Mama paused as her voice caught. "It . . . it simply hurts too much."

Pa gathered Mama into his arms and held her gently. He wiped a tear from the corner of Mama's eye. Betsy held her breath. Would Pa agree to return to Pennsylvania?

"I know, I know," he whispered. "And there's nothing back East for me." He shook his head. "Humph," he admitted softly. "Nothing except my whole life." He hugged Mama closer.

"I know you haven't changed your mind about returning East," Mama said sadly. "What are we going to do?"

Betsy didn't have any ideas, so she

didn't know what to say. Perhaps that was just as well. She knew better than to interrupt her parents during a serious discussion. Besides, it seemed as if they'd forgotten her, and Betsy always learned the most about life when adults didn't remember she was listening.

"I don't know," Pa replied to Mama's helpless question. "Can't we at least talk it over? The stagecoach doesn't leave for a few days anyway."

Mama gazed up into Pa's eyes. She smiled softly.

"Yes, I suppose it won't do any harm to discuss the matter," she agreed.

Pa bent and kissed Mama again, then he quickly straightened.

"Well, there's no time like right now, I reckon," he said. "Betsy, girl, you get yourself ready and get to bed. Your mama and I have much to think about."

"Bed!" Betsy gasped. "But, Pa! It's still daylight!"

"Betsy," Pa said in his no-nonsense voice.

"Yes, Pa," Betsy mumbled, and the three of them hurried to the house.

Betsy quickly changed her clothes, kissed her parents goodnight, and scurried off to bed, careful to keep her door ajar so she could overhear the conversation. She didn't really feel guilty for trying to listen. After all, *her* future depended on her parents' decision, too.

"How about a cool drink of water, Lydie?" Betsy heard Pa say. "Or I could fix a pot of coffee."

"Water's fine," Mama said. "Let me help you."

Betsy heard the clang of tin cups,

then a long silent pause, followed by a soft giggle. She heard the ladle bump the side of the water bucket and a splash as one of her parents dipped the drinks.

"I suppose the mine is doing quite well if you could send Betsy a gold nugget worth a trip across the country," Mama said, her voice growing louder as she headed into the sitting room.

"Yes," Pa replied. "It's doing very well."

"I just still can't believe that Betsy did such a thing, running off on her own," Mama added. "You've no idea how worried and heartsick I was!"

"Yes," Pa said. "I do have an idea."

"Of course, I'm sorry. She's your daughter, too," Mama said.

Betsy squirmed in her bed. She really hadn't meant to worry them. But she'd done just fine, after all.

"Well, that's all just water under the bridge," said Pa.

The sound of his boots grew louder and louder until Betsy realized he was right outside her bedroom door. She closed her eyes as fast as she could.

"I think it'd be a might nicer outside on the porch, don't you, Lydie?" he asked, and Betsy was certain she could hear laughter in his voice.

"Yes," Mama agreed. "I believe there's a cool breeze this evening."

"Most surely," Pa said, chuckling. He slowly pulled Betsy's bedroom door shut, but he seemed to raise his voice slightly before it closed. "The porch is nice and cool and a might more pri-vate, too, I reckon."

Fiddlesticks! Betsy thought. The fading sound of Mama's laughter drifted through the house, and the clunk of Pa's boots echoed as he headed toward the front door.

chapter
ELEVEN

BETSY was certain she would not sleep. How could she? Not when her parents were sitting on the porch this very moment and deciding their future!

Betsy smiled smugly. True, her idea hadn't exactly worked out as she originally had planned, but it had worked nonetheless. Her mama and pa were together, talking, and that was really the main purpose of her whole trip. Perhaps now that she was here,

Mama would face her grief. Or it might only get worse. Betsy shook her head to clear away her doubts. There was no use fretting about it.

She looked around her bedroom at the comforting log walls, the smooth plank floor, the evening sun shining in a long streak through the window. Whatever happened, she had enjoyed her brief visit here. But now that she'd seen Pa again, how could she bear to leave him? How could Mama bear to leave him again?

Betsy rolled onto her back and stared at the ceiling. Sleep? No, Betsy was sure she would not get a moment's rest that night.

But before she knew what had happened, she felt a gentle shaking as Pa wakened her. She glanced around until she saw Mama holding a lamp.

Her face looked tired.

"Wake up, Betsy," Pa said, shaking Betsy again.

Betsy bolted upright in her bed, all sleep wiped from her mind. She couldn't read her parents' expressions. And the lamp Mama held meant it was still dark outside.

"Your mama and I have been talking all night. We've reached a decision," Pa said. "We wanted to tell you right away."

Betsy glanced at her Mama. Fear squeezed her heart. Was the news good or bad? Oh, she simply couldn't bear bad news.

"Mama?" she whispered, her voice shaking a bit.

Mama set the lamp on the small bedside table and sat beside Betsy. She hugged her daughter tightly.

"Oh, Betsy," she said, chuckling. "Don't look so worried. The news is good."

Betsy sighed loud, and Pa laughed, joining them on the edge of Betsy's bed.

"Are . . . are we staying in California?" Betsy asked her Mama.

"No," answered Mama.

Betsy stared wide-eyed at Pa. "Are we all going back to Pennsylvania?" she asked.

"Heavens, no!" Pa said.

"But, but," Betsy began, fear gripping her chest once more. Hadn't Mama said the news was good? "But what else is there? We are . . . we are staying to—" she was almost afraid to ask, but she plunged ahead, "We are staying together, aren't we?"

"Yes, we certainly are," Pa said,

wrapping one arm around Mama and the other around Betsy. "For always, this time," he added firmly.

Betsy slipped her hand into Mama's. She had no idea what had been decided, but she felt a strange excitement building inside of her. Her eyes began to sparkle as she sat quietly, waiting for her pa to continue.

"We've decided to sell the house and gold claim," Pa said. "I've had my fill of mining, and I've got a nice little savings set aside, too. I'd like to try my hand at farming, I think, and your mama's agreed to try it with me. What do you say, Betsy? How does packing up and moving north to the Oregon Territory sound? There's land aplenty for the taking. Good, rich farming land."

Betsy's mouth opened wide. She couldn't have been more surprised if

Pa had told her they were all turning to street vending! Farming! Animals and crops and grassy meadows. Perhaps a pond with ducklings and a barn with cute, fuzzy lambs. She liked that idea just fine!

She let out a giant whoop.

"When? When are we leaving?" she asked, a little breathless.

"Hold on!" Pa replied, laughing. "Not till spring." Pa began to count on his fingers. "That's eight months. We need to sell this place, pack and buy supplies for our trip, not to mention your mama writing to your grandmama to send your belongings out here."

"I want you to write to Grandmama, too, Betsy," Mama interjected. "To thank her for allowing us to stay with her this past year."

Betsy looked at her mama, her eyes

shining with joy. "I will, Mama, I will," she promised. She couldn't believe it! Everything had turned out so much better than she had dreamed.

Pa cleared his throat and his face grew serious. "We'll do all that on one condition, Betsy," he said.

Betsy looked into his solemn face. She held her breath. Pa pulled Mama and Betsy close until the three of them sat in a tight circle on Betsy's bed. Mama reached out and held Betsy's chin in her soft hand.

"You must promise you'll never do anything like this again, Betsy," said Ma. "Running off—for whatever reason, good or bad—never solves any problem. I've learned that now, too. And even though this time there is a happy ending, something truly terrible might have happened to you. Your pa and I thank the good Lord for keeping you safe and for bringing us all to- gether again."

"I promise, Mama," Betsy said. She reached up and gave each of her parents a hard hug. "I'm so sorry I worried you."

"Very well," Pa said. "It's finished— we'll put it behind us and go on from here."

Betsy giggled and raised her hand, pointing her finger into the air.

"On to Oregon!" she shouted, then joined her parents in laughter and another warm hug.

about the
author

CANDRI HODGES has always loved to read. As a little girl, she usually had her nose "stuck in a book." As an adult, she especially enjoys reading historical stories, but she often finds herself wondering: What was the child in the story thinking? So Mrs. Hodges likes to write historical books telling the child's side of the story.

Mrs. Hodges lives in Felton, Pennsylvania, with her husband, son, and two dogs. Her favorite activities are cross-stitching and antique shopping. And, of course, she loves reading and writing.